Class Three at Sea

To Pippa Gerrett and intrepid teachers everywhere! —JJ
For Kit —LC

First American edition published in 2008 by Lerner Publishing Group, Inc.

Published by arrangement with Hodder Children's Books,
a division of Hachette Children's Books, London, England

Text copyright © 2008 by Julia Jarman
Illustrations copyright © 2008 by Lynne Chapman

Carolrhoda Books
A division of Lerner Publishing Group, Inc.
241 First Avenue North
Minneapolis, MN 55401 U.S.A.

Website address: www.lernerbooks.com

Library of Congress Cataloging-in-Publication Data

Jarman, Julia.
    Class Three at sea/ by Julia Jarman ; illustrated by Lynne Chapman.
        p.   cm.
    Summary: The teacher and students of Class Three are so absorbed by the marine life they
see while sailing on the ocean that they do not notice that they are being pursued by pirates.
    ISBN 978–0–8225–7617–4 (trade hard cover : alk. paper)
    [1. Stories in rhyme. 2. Ocean—Fiction. 3. Marine animals—Fiction.
4. Pirates—Fiction. 5. School field trips—Fiction. 6. Humorous stories.]
I. Chapman, Lynne, 1960- ill. II. Title. III. Title: Class 3 at sea.
PZ8.3.J2746Clh 2008
[E]—dc22
                                                    2007042656

Printed and bound in China
1 2 3 4 5 6—OS—13 12 11 10 09 08

Class Three
AT SEA

Julia Jarman

Illustrations by
Lynne Chapman

CAROLRHODA BOOKS · MINNEAPOLIS · NEW YORK

On the day Class Three went to sea,
they saw donkeys dancing joyfully.

They saw some sea lions skipping stones.

But they didn't see . . .

...the SKULL and CROSSBONES.

They heard
Teacher say,
"Wear a life jacket."
"Listen to me!"
and "Stop that racket!"

They saw some seagulls plop, plop, plopping, but they didn't hear . . .

. . . the pirates plotting.

They saw some dolphins near the shore, doing math. "2 plus 2 is 4."

They saw two pelicans sniff and sneer.

But they didn't see the pirates . . .

... getting
near.

They saw Octopus tied up in knots,
and they untied him. "Thanks a lot!"

They saw fishes flying in the sky, as Octopus waved,

"Good-bye! Good-bye!"

But they didn't see . . .

...**Hairy Legs**
board the ship.

They didn't
see him
GRAB Phillip.

They didn't see
Pirate Booger Nose

**grab Jackie,
James, and
Jenny Rose.**

They didn't see **Pirate Fish Breath Frank** make poor Lenny **WALK THE PLANK**.

Or the chief called **Rotten Teeth**
grab the captain, whose name was **Keith.**

"See that island up ahead?
Sail straight to it, or **Class Three's dead!**"

The chief had a map with
a spot marked **X**.
Percy saw it
with his specs!

Class Three's teacher didn't see.
She was perched on a
pirate's knee.

But...

. . . **Lucky Lenny,**

swimming the crawl,

hitched a lift from Porpoise,

playing ball.

Porpoise took him *very fast*

to Octopus,
who was **aghast**.

"**Quick!**" he cried to his big brother. "One good turn deserves another."

But time, alas, was running out—
for **Rotten Teeth**,
the smelly lout,

yelled,

"I AM GETTING VERY CROSS!"

as the captain stuttered, "I th-think we're lost."

Then all of a sudden,
they heard a whoosh!
followed by
a mighty

sploosh!

As Octopus landed, then his brother,
they grabbed one pirate, then **another**.

"You'd better let go of Class Three," Lenny said, as Rotten Teeth's eyes **POPPED** out of his head.

The trembling pirates
fled the ship—all except
for **Pirate Pip**.
"Miss and me,
we'd like to marry."

"Later," said Pat and Pete and Harry,
for they'd seen something
by the light of the moon . . .

Treasure Island!
"Not a moment too soon!"

Harry spied
the spot marked **X**.
His telescope saw
every speck.

"Sail straight onward, Captain Keith.
And try to miss that coral reef!"

Very soon they reached
their goal, where Class Three
dug a very deep hole.

And at the bottom—yes, you've guessed—

they found a stuffed-full treasure chest!

So if ever your class goes to sea,
remember what happened to Class Three.
And if pirates board, don't make a fuss . . .

just make friends
with an octopus!